MIDDLEMARK
Issue n° 17 — Winter 2021/22

GW01044245

PART 1

On the cover, legendary artist MARK LECKEY is photographed by Mark Peckmezian.

Library key 5
Snippets 6
The Interview: MARK LECKEY 8
    by Hari Kunzru — *'To be honest, I'm looking for a way out of the art world.'*
Supernatural bookshelf 33

PART 2

The Book of the Season is MIDDLEMARCH: A STUDY OF PROVINCIAL LIFE by Mary Ann Evans who, for reasons of societal sexism, wrote under the pen name George Eliot.

Welcome to Websville 36
George Eliot reads the news 37
    by Rebecca Mead — *Railways, cholera, covid, kindness*
My twenties, my thirties, my forties... 39
    by Rob Palk — *The success world is not my world*
Some times I set a good example 44
    by Jean Hannah Edelstein — *My life as a moral model*
Middlemarch, 2022 46
Book club with old friend who happens to be a film star . . . 55
    by Deborah Friedell — *Three-act reread with the brilliant Jordana Brewster*
Speed read 60
Two wills, burn one 61
    by Yelena Moskovich — *Very small inheritance story*
Education sex 62
    by Tara Isabella Burton — *Submission fetish but for scholars*
Letters 65
Summer book reveal 66
Issue timeline 68

Typography from an 1871 first edition of *Middlemarch*.

Curvilinear view of the Edouard Loewy Bookstore in Paris, as captured by ANDRÉ KERTÉSZ. The son of a Budapest bookseller, Kertész created countless images relating to books and reading.

Library Key

Each category in the Dewey Decimal System
represents a lifetime of possible investigation

(011) Bibliographies
(030) Encyclopedic works
(096) Books notable for bindings
(098) Prohibited works, forgeries, and hoaxes
(123) Determinism and indeterminism
(135) Dreams and mysteries
(145) Sensationalism
(167) Hypotheses
(173) Ethics of family relationships
(188) Stoicism
(198) Philosophy of Russia
(239) Apologetics and polemics
(295) Zoroastrianism
(307) Communities
(316) General statistics of Africa
(324) The political process
(359) Sea forces
(366) Secret associations and societies
(367) General clubs
(368) Insurance
(383) Postal communication
(391) Costume and personal appearance
(393) Death customs
(469) Portuguese
(513) Arithmetic
(520) Astronomy
(548) Crystallography
(592) Invertebrates
(611) Human anatomy
(604) Technical drawing
(622) Mining
(636) Animal husbandry

(638) Insect culture
(648) Housekeeping
(653) Shorthand
(663) Beverage technology
(687) Clothing and accessories
(697) Heating, ventilating, air conditioning
(709) History of the arts
(715) Woody plants in landscape architecture
(747) Interior decoration
(748) Glass
(750) Painting and paintings
(761) Block printing
(777) Cinematography and videography
(783) Music for single voices
(795) Games of chance
(808) Rhetoric
(823) English fiction
(835) German speeches
(915) Geography of Asia
(989) History of Uruguay
(999) Extraterrestrial worlds

THE HAPPY READER — Bookish Magazine — Issue n° 17
A collaboration between Penguin Books and Fantastic Man

EDITOR-IN-CHIEF Seb Emina ART DIRECTOR Tom Etherington MANAGING EDITOR Maria Bedford
EDITORIAL DIRECTORS Jop van Bennekom, Gert Jonkers PICTURE RESEARCH Frances Roper ADDITIONAL
DESIGN Matthew Young PRODUCTION Ilaria Rovera MARKETING Liz Parsons BRAND DIRECTOR Sam Voulters
MARKETING DIRECTOR Ingrid Matts PUBLISHER Stefan McGrath CONTRIBUTORS Florence Arnold, Tara Isabella
Burton, Jean Hannah Edelstein, Deborah Friedell, Ben Grimes, Jordan Kelly, Hari Kunzru, Jamie MacRae, Tiago Martins,
Rebecca Mead, Yelena Moskovich, Rob Palk, Mark Peckmezian, Marton Perlaki. THANK YOU Eliot Haworth,
Emily King, Peter Law, Pete Pawsey, Oscar Rickett, Natalie Whittle, Anna Wilson.

PENGUIN BOOKS 20 Vauxhall Bridge Road London SW1V 2SA info@thehappyreader.com www.thehappyreader.com

Snippets

Riveting news for book lovers,
compiled by our editor-in-chief

The Haruki Murakami Library has opened in Tokyo. Located at Waseda University, where Murakami once studied theatre, the library was designed by architect Kengo Kuma to house the author's personal archive plus tens of thousands of his vinyl records. Well, it's a bit of a Murakami theme park: there's also a replica of the author's desk and a café serving his favourite coffee. 'I wish a place like this had been built after my death, so I can rest in peace and have someone take care of it,' said Murakami, 72, at the building's launch event. 'I feel a bit nervous seeing it while I'm still alive.'

In library-land in general, big change is afoot. New research shows if there's no fine to pay for late returns, readers are less likely to hang on to the library's copy of, say, Charles Dickens' *Little Dorrit*. It's an insight that's led libraries in New York, Chicago and Boston to abandon all such penalties. 'Unfortunately, fines are quite effective at preventing our most vulnerable communities from using our branches,' admitted New York Library president Tony Marx. Meanwhile, in Northern Ireland, around 87,000 overdue fines have been wiped from the record in an extraordinary post-pandemic amnesty.

A new kind of book has been invented, one which can be disposed of by planting it in the ground. Pioneered by a company named Willsow, each is both about a vegetable and impregnated with seeds for that vegetable. You read the book (*The Lettuce Who Wanted a New Look* is one), then bury it in the garden, then, after a bit of a wait, you meet, and, yes, eat, the main character.

Life lacking a plaything? Author Sophie Heawood recommends acquiring a doll version of Kurt Vonnegut, American writer of many cult classics, most famously *Slaughterhouse-Five*. The soft toy is imbued, she reckons, with limitless morale-boosting powers thanks to the reminder it offers of Vonnegut's work, wisdom and generosity of spirit. In Heawood's case, custody of the doll, made by a company called Little Thinkers, is shared with her ten-year-old daughter. 'I'm not sure I'd have got through all those early years of single parenthood if we hadn't had a teddy of Kurt Vonnegut,' she says.

The one hundredth anniversary of James Joyce's *Ulysses* is upon us. The actual date is 2 February but it's a literary centenary of such weight that the whole year is to be one long act of tribute-making. Happenings include a major exhibition at the Morgan Library in New York City; another at the Harry Ransom Center in Austin, Texas; myriad goings-on at Shakespeare & Company, the Paris bookshop that originally published the novel; talks, readings, exhibitions, shows and so on at manifold Dublin venues. But amid this world buffet of Joycean delectables, be honest: have you actually read it? Now is the time! Hold to the now!

According to a study published in volume 164 of the journal *Social Science & Medicine*, people who voraciously read books live for around two years longer than those who don't. Before you ask, other readable media, including this magazine, do not bestow the same benefit. 'Book reading contributed to a survival advantage that was significantly greater than that observed for reading newspapers or magazines,' said the study's authors.

Glasgow indie Outwith Books had a surprise lunchtime visit from a burly security operative in spivvy shoes followed shortly afterwards by Nicola Sturgeon, the famously bibliophilic Scottish leader whose constituency office is a few streets away. Her haul included *Harlem Shuffle* by Colson Whitehead, *Summerwater* by Sarah Moss and *News of the Dead* by James Robertson. She also praised Maggie Shipstead's 'multi-layered' *Great Circle* and sounded slightly ambivalent about the cult of Sally Rooney.

Not long after 'semi-separating' from outspoken billionaire Elon Musk, bookish pop star Grimes was photographed sitting on the ground on an LA sidewalk. Her back up against a fence, she was immersed in a copy of Karl Marx's *Communist Manifesto*. The headlines wrote themselves: 'Grimes seen reading Karl Marx following split with world's richest man,' went one. A few days later she posted a statement to a social media platform saying it was just a performance for the media, going on to clarify, 'I am not a communist (although there are some very smart ideas in this book but personally I'm more interested in a radical decentralised UBI [universal basic income] that I think could potentially be achieved thru crypto and gaming).' Now why didn't Marx think of that?

Recording artist MC Hammer, famous for the 1990 song 'U Can't Touch This', is a fan of G. W. F. Hegel, particularly citing the German philosopher's 1807 work *The Phenomenology of Spirit*.

Readers are reminded that this magazine has a monthly email newsletter, which is simply entitled *Happy Readings*. Written by me, it's a kind of mini *THR* in your inbox, offering more in the way of Snippets-style news items plus exclusive interviews with notable readers and an exploration of a classic Book of the Month. Sign up for free at thehappyreader.com/newsletter.

Mark Leckey

The artist as ravenous consumer of horror books, political books, small fragments of poetry... This issue's cover interview offers an illuminating journey into the mind of one of the most influential artists at work today.

    MARK LECKEY was born in 1964 to a working class family in Birkenhead, England. He went to art school in Newcastle then, among other things, ran a clothing stall in Notting Hill and played in a rock band before finding fame as an artist at the end of the '90s, going on to win the Turner Prize in 2008. One of the few genuinely unpretentious people in the art world, Leckey has lately been described as 'the artist of the YouTube generation'. A few months before the pandemic put the world on pause, his importance was galvanised in a must-see Tate Britain installation involving a life-size replica of a motorway bridge; he opens 2022 a short walk across the Thames from there with a new solo show at Cabinet Gallery in Vauxhall.

In conversation with
HARI KUNZRU

Portraits by
MARK PECKMEZIAN

MARK LECKEY

BRITAIN

In 1999, Mark Leckey's film *Fiorucci Made Me Hardcore* tore through the art world. Its spectral images of Northern Soul dancers and dissected rave soundscape captured what Leckey has described as an 'anguish', the feelings of loss and yearning that run through the exhilaration of British dance culture. In films, performances, installations and events in the last twenty years, Leckey has explored ways of speaking and seeing through the archive, assembling shards of sound and image into the elements of an unusually supple and wide-ranging aesthetic language. His work is marked by a wry humour, and a way of mining critical thought from the detritus of the ordinary: he has confronted monumental sculpture with a monumental stack of bass bins. He's exorcised a motorway bridge.

Leckey says, self-deprecatingly, that he's 'mired in the past', but his acute connection to memory and his autobiographical knack of making his own experiences stand for larger tendencies in the culture have made him one of the most celebrated British artists of his generation. He won the Turner Prize in 2008 and his work has been collected by major museums. These days he lives in north London. When we spoke, he was finishing a new film, *To the Old World (Thank You for the Use of Your Body)*, so it could be shown in New York. I'd just watched and rewatched his 2015 film, *Dream English Kid 1964–1999AD*, which had absorbed me so much that I'd ended up making a sort of blow-by-blow list of its various beats and references: *Carry On*, fishnets, pixels, the three-day week, bar fires, Joy Division, Luther Vandross, Profondo Rosso, Campari, nuclear war...

HARI: When you were growing up, were there books in your house?
    MARK: No.

H: What reading matter was there? In *Dream English Kid*, you gave a nod to the *Radio Times*.
    M: Yeah. And my dad had one of those Wilbur Smith books. And who was the other one at that time? Alistair MacLean, was it?

H: My dad liked those. I read a lot of Alistair MacLean as a kid.

M: That's all my dad had. My mum didn't read at all. My dad barely read. The first things I really remember getting into were *The Hobbit*, *Lord of the Rings*.

H: So did you go on being interested in fantasy, in escaping to other worlds?

M: I went more towards horror. I read and watch horror for comfort. It's like sausage and mash.

H: What's comforting about horror?

M: I don't know. As soon as the kids go out, that's what I want to do. I'll watch a zombie film tonight, just to... I don't know. I just find it very comforting. I guess it's to do with getting a VCR when I was about fifteen, sixteen, and getting those early horror films, those video nasties. There's this sort of illicit thrill. You could get hold of those videos and that was very exciting.

H: What about the books — was it James Herbert? Was that somebody you liked?

M: Yeah. And I read all the Stephen King books. I love Stephen King. But then I read the more... I'm not alone with this, right?

H: No. I mean, it's a hugely popular genre. But comfort is such an odd word to use, because clearly they're about discomfort.

M: Familiarity, I guess. It's like goths, isn't it? There's something very domestic about goths. They're outside in nature, but you know they just want to curl up on the couch. And I've got a bit of that in me. I don't know why I find it comforting. Sometimes I read stuff to engage my mind and then I read stuff to switch it off. But there's very sophisticated horror. I just reread Colson Whitehead, *Zone One*.

H: More zombies.

M: There's a lot going on in that book. And [Mark Danielewski's] *House of Leaves* is another one like it.

H: That's a discomforting book, isn't it? All the conventions break down. You get lost in the maze of that book.

M: In the same way that you would in fantasy. There are a lot of good young female horror writers at the moment. I've enjoyed a lot of them. Let me think. *Come Closer*, Sara Gran; *Good Neighbours*, Sarah Langan; *All Things Cease to Appear*, Elizabeth Brundage; *The Last House on Needless Street*, Catriona Ward; *Sisters*, Daisy Johnson; *The Animals in That Country*, Laura Jean McKay; *The Lamplighters*,

Leckey, his wife
and two children live
in north London.

Emma Stonex. There's more. I'll have to look them up. Trouble is, because I read everything on a Kindle, I don't remember anyone's name or the name of the book because it's not there. I hate to tell you this.

H: That's OK.
M: I don't like that sort of Clive Barker horror.

H: I've never read Clive Barker.
M: What was that film? *Hellraiser*.

H: Oh yeah. So is that because it's more supernatural? What makes a horror story comforting?
M: No, it's more — it's all flayed bodies these days. Pulling the body apart in order to read its entrails. I don't go there. It's probably too visceral for me. That's not what I'm looking for.

H: So, when you—
M: On the verge of slapstick I want. *Scooby-Doo*.

H: There are whole bits of my brain that I'm sure were programmed by episodes of *Scooby-Doo*. That's also exactly the kind of media image I can imagine you taking and using. You're clearly a collector and you're an assembler of pre-existing stuff to make meaning happen between all these elements. Do you actually collect in any kind of formal way? Do you have a really great record collection with everything in plastic sleeves? Or do you just have a pile of bits that you root through?
M: I just have a pile of bits. All those energies have gone into the videos. I think if I hadn't made the videos, I probably would have collections, but it all goes into this. I'm just trying to understand what's produced me. Do you know what I mean? I'm not remarking on that mediation. That's what *Dream English Kid* is.

H: It's a sort of video autobiography. And you start it in the year of your birth, 1964. One of the elements you include is Harold Wilson's voice, as he gives the famous speech about the 'white heat of technology'. And we see an empty motorway, and a bridge, that we'll gradually see decaying, getting covered with graffiti, as time goes on. But first we see it through the back window of a car, a child's view. At one point you even show us this dream motorway through the heated back windscreen, where bands of condensation striate the image, and sort of louvre it, send it further into modernist abstraction. And I remember that exact experience so strongly, looking through the bars of moisture on the car window. That went in very deep for me. I wanted to ask you about a tone that I see in your work, and I see in the work

1. GOG AND MAGOG
—

The words Gog and Magog appear frequently throughout a number of religious texts, although there remains little consensus on who, or what, they refer to. Both have been said to be descriptors of: a place, a person, a people, enemies of the Messiah and attackers of Alexander the Great. Who knows. There is, for sure, a Gog Magog Golf Course, roughly four miles south of Cambridge.

of other people who grew up at the same time as us. A sort of lamentation. There was a sort of promise made when we were children, made by the culture around us, the promise of a rational, shared society that we were told we'd grow up into but which was totally ripped away by the time we became adults. I wonder about your relationship to that version of the future that never came?

M: I've never thought of that before, the idea of a future promise. I think I've always just taken it as a given that that's the way the world should be and it got wrecked. It's like, that's the world that was destroyed. Especially in the North-west, where I grew up, you literally saw that shit pulled down. Do you know what I mean? It was levelled. You physically watched that stuff just rot and ruin.

H: At one point, in your audio piece *Exorcism of the Bridge @ Eastham Rake*, which features the same motorway bridge that punctuates *Dream English Kid*, you're leading a chant, and you seem to be ridding yourself of the corpse of the twentieth century. 'Out! Indwelling spirits, stagnant entities of dank decades... Out, colossus of post-war consensus struck with paralysis' — this is after invoking a mystical list of names including Gog and Magog, Robin Goodfellow and... Barbara Castle. And that's another element, maybe. That this post-war behemoth was already crumbling, and we live in the ruins, and we need to throw it off to move on.

M: It's really accelerated in the last two years, the sense I have now of belonging to an entirely other period. And those values, like I said, I've always taken as a given in some way, and now I realise that they were conditional. It was a very brief moment, actually. To me, it seemed like a long post-war boom, but actually it was only two decades, really, wasn't it? And then it was gone. I think in a way that rave was the end of that. We carried our generation, carried those ideals, and tried to repeat them in the ruins with the debris and all the rest of it.

H: One of the things that drive these videos, drive all your work really, is music. How did you get your information about music when you were growing up? For our generation it was all about the newsprint music weeklies like *Melody Maker* and the *NME*? Did you read them?

M: Yeah. Yeah, it was *NME*, *Sounds*. I saw a lot of stuff in *Sounds*.

H: And are you a big liner notes guy?

M: No. Not really. I mean I read them but I'm... I'm not a music geek. I just read this book called *You're History: The Twelve Strangest Women In Music*, by Lesley Chow. So it talks about twelve different singers from Rihanna to Kate Bush. She talks about Rihanna's

Leckey has always been
interested in ancient civilisa-
tions and the notion that we
are, in fact, still living in one.

'Umbrella'. She basically says there's no way of writing about 'Umbrella' using that kind of *Sounds*, *NME* music-criticism vocabulary. When I listen to music I'm not looking for an artwork that can be unpacked. I'm looking for something that makes you hot and bothered, and kind of confused, disorientated, right? Or joyful. I get very bored of geeky music conversation. I would have started reading the music press when I was about thirteen. I remember punk coming along in the music press. Then I suppose I was taking it really, really seriously around when I was sixteen, seventeen, so post-punk, '79, '80. I think I read it up to about '83 and then I got bored of it.

H: I remember that the writers would be dropping a lot of references to French theory and situationism and all this kind of thing. For me, that was my introduction to some of these ideas.

M: Yeah. Definitely. I was in Ellesmere Port, which is quite a small town. We had to go to Liverpool to get anything — I had to cross over the Mersey. So you know, I mean this is already clichéd, but you're searching this stuff out and so there's a kind of excitement about that. It was quite mystical. Some of this stuff would — I would be scared by it. I remember being very scared by Crass, even though I went to see them. I found them kind of satanic. My first introduction to Marx was Scritti Politti, because they talked about Gramsci. Scritti Politti — I can't remember the connection.

[Neither Hari nor Mark remember that the band's name was a deliberate misspelling of Gramsci's Scritti Politici, 'Political Writings'.]

H: Scritti Politti. I remember, they were very intellectual. They were dropping Derrida references.

M: Yeah, and I wanted to understand who all these people were. And that would mean a trip to the library.

H: Would you be able to find that kind of thing in the library? Were you confident enough to ask people?

M: It wasn't like I went to the library and read Marx. I'd like to say I did. I was a fourteen-year-old and I read the *Beano* or whatever. At school, the idea of information or history was dead. That was a dead area. At the school I went to, there was no thrill in education. And it was scorned. You know what I mean? Me and my peers were scornful of education so I wasn't interested in school particularly. At first I was, then it got knocked out of me. So, music was like a way back into it.

H: You ended up wanting to make art and going to art school. And so what sort of exposure to that art culture did you have? Were you reading books about painting?

M: There's two reasons I went to art school. One is, I mean this used to be the case, I don't know if it is any more, but essentially people who went to art school could draw. It was like you had some talent, some facility for drawing, so that would take you on a path to art school. So I could draw. As a kid I used to draw a lot. I went late to art school — I went as a mature student because I left school and was on the dole for four years. I was getting into trouble. I was a kind of delinquent. And my stepdad persuaded me to go to art school. He was a dock worker. He sat me down and said, 'Everything in this room where we sit has at one point been drawn. Someone sketched it out. Someone has put pencil to paper and thought this out.' And he's going, 'You could do this. This is something you could do.' And so I went to Foundation. I had to go back and do my A levels, which is a long process, but basically I got a full grant. I got housing benefit, I got a maintenance grant because I was older—

H: Where did you do your Foundation?

M: Foundation I did at Liverpool. And then my BA I did in Newcastle at the poly. But I wasn't really thinking that much about art. I wanted to be a muralist. If Banksy had been around when I was in my late teens, that's where I would have gone. But more than that, I wanted to be in a band. I went to art school to find some like-minded people that I could form a band with. Because I tried to be in a band in my home town and it was very disappointing.

H: Tell me about it!

M: I don't blame it on them. When I went in the eighties, it wasn't that far from the sixties in terms of The Who and all the rest of it. And then that trajectory had carried on through McLaren and I'm trying to think who else — Bowie and all the rest of them.

H: Roxy Music. There used to be a working-class intellectual culture that came out of British art schools but that seems to have been — almost deliberately — smashed up in the last generation or so. The path that you had, I guess, has been very more or less blocked off now.

M: Yeah. Completely. I teach at art schools and it's very apparent. You don't get many of me at art school now.

H: Bands are posher than they used to be and artists are posher than they used to be.

M: But then people still manage it somehow. I'm always amazed and very impressed with how people do it. A lot of people just say,

'Fuck it' to the debt they're going to incur and they just go. I'm reading a book by Cynthia Cruz called *The Melancholia of Class*. It's an American book, but yeah, that's definitely on my wavelength. She's describing this condition that comes with moving from the working class or to the middle class, to the bourgeoisie. And how that leaves a kind of, well, it's more than sadness, a kind of loss.

H: Did you ever read 'Digging', the famous Seamus Heaney poem where he's watching his dad in the garden, and he's really feeling the distance between them? He's there with his pen, writing his poem, and his dad is cutting turf, and the distance feels unbridgeable. It sounds like what you're describing. The boy who went off and got educated and realised he can't ever quite come home again.

M: I'd like to read more of him, because there's one he wrote called 'St Kevin and the Blackbird'. St Kevin is an anchorite, and he has his hands out in prayer and a bird comes and makes a nest and he has to stay there, holding out his hands. Seamus is describing this work. And then he says, 'And since the whole thing's imagined anyhow / Imagine being Kevin.' Which is a brilliant move. A twist.

H: What did you get exposed to at art school that meant you ended up doing what you've done rather than industrial design?

M: There were a lot of hippies there. Well, crusties from down south who didn't want to go to London colleges so they go off to Newcastle or Edinburgh. So there was quite a hippy vibe there. And then in the second year, so this is like '87, the second year, this sort of Goldsmiths programme made its way up north. The first year we had Gombrich's book *The Story of Art*. And it was like, 'There you go.' Suddenly we begin the second year, it's Hal Foster, Roland Barthes, all of this. It's like year zero, it's Pol Pot — when you start again. And it really fucked me up, basically. Well, not fucked me up. It messed with my mind.

H: In a bad way?

M: Yeah. I guess, yeah. I couldn't grasp it. I mean, my best friend at college was a Geordie miner, a Marxist Geordie miner. He grasped all this stuff instinctively. I couldn't. I just couldn't. I had no experience of reading at that level. To me, it's always seemed a very brutal thing to do actually, to try and instil that in you so coldly.

H: But you clearly got to a point where the music culture, counter-culture stuff connected to the high-theory stuff. And then you were off to the races.

M: I still read theory at a very superficial level. I *glean* it. If there's

All Images: courtesy the artist and Cabinet, London

Selected video works in chronological order. Row 1–3: *Fiorucci Made Me Hardcore*, 1999, 14 minutes 30 seconds. Row 4–6: *Dream English Kid, 1964–1999 AD*, 2015, 23 minutes.

19

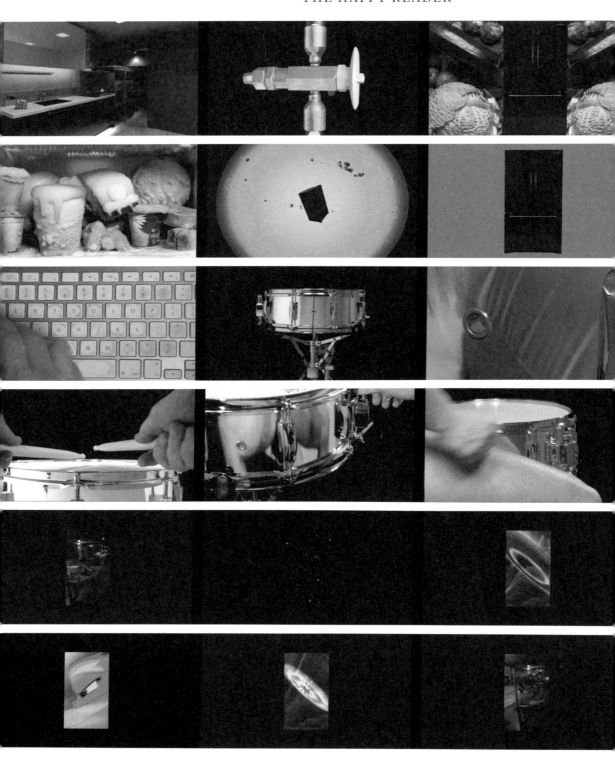

Row 1–2: *GreenScreenRefridgeratorAction*, 2010, 17 minutes 9 seconds. Row 3–4: *Pearl Vision*, 2012, 3 minutes 6 seconds. Row 5–6: *Under Armour in the Twilight Sparkle*, 2021, 4 minutes 15 seconds. Watch Leckey's videos at Youtube.com/MrLeckey. Listen to Leckey's radio show at nts.live.

anything there that tickles my fancy, then I... You know what? You see this in a lot of artists: it's like badly digested theory can actually produce some interesting ideas. Whereas often perfectly assimilated theory can produce very airless ideas.

H: I agree. If you're using theory to try and explain the world then you need to understand it in a systematic way, but misrecognitions are really useful in creative work. And there is a sense in which stoned half-reading of difficult books is actually more useful than the systematic, academic reading of them.

M: The biggest problem I have with it in terms of my own history with it was the shibboleths that are kind of stuck with me. When making videos, the objective was to make it non-narrative. And I'd be like, 'Why?'

H: It's interesting to hear you say that the art orthodoxy is anti-narrative. There's a difference between a lot of my artist friends and a lot of my writer friends. I remember talking about *Game of Thrones*, and all the writers were watching it. They could bracket all the crap about it and then just get into the baroqueness of the storyline. The artists (and this is a generalisation, of course) hated it. There are these different creative cultures that have concretised around whether you think narrative is absorbing or something a bit embarrassing and crass.

M: During the pandemic, one thing I did was write a treatment. For years, I've wanted to make an adaption of *The Invention of Morel* by Adolfo Bioy Casares. So this has been going on for a long time and someone else wrote it and it didn't work and then I had a go. So I wrote a treatment and my lack of interest in narrative made it very difficult. Because I was thinking very visually. I really struggled with the idea of a compelling story. I'd have these conversations with Film4 and I'd be like, 'Really? What, he's got to do something heroic?'

H: Why did you want to make a film?

M: Money. But I mean, to be honest, I'm also looking for a way out of the art world.

H: Really?

M: Yeah. I kind of want out.

H: But you've done so well. They love you in the art world. You're best at art.

M: The trouble is, if you're loved in the art world, that love basically carries you to a super-yacht moored off Venice, do you know what I mean? And I don't want that. I don't want to go there.

All Images: courtesy the artist and Cabinet, London

His pyjama-esque outfit
suggests a cosy and
unhurried reading life.

H: I guess the lifestyle of the ultra-rich is very far from the concerns of your work. It's been moving to me to watch some of your films again, because your work is wrapped up with a version of Englishness and a version of an English childhood and teenage years that I recognise and identify with. You've articulated structures of feeling that I haven't seen articulated anywhere else. I'm thinking, for example, of a video clip you found of a guy crashing through the glass wall of a bus stop. You've used him twice, in a work called *In This Lingering Twilight Sparkle* and again in one called *To the Old World (Thank You for the Use of Your Body)*. It's a cell phone video. There's no context. Maybe he's doing it as a dare. It doesn't look like an accident. It looks as if he's doing it deliberately, running at this bus stop and crashing through the glass. You repeat it again and again. Sometimes we just hear the sound. There's a disbelieving audience reaction. Somebody says, 'What a fucking run.' It's destructive and stupid. It's transgressive and pointless but it's also funny. And somehow very English. That connection between violence and humour. Is that a thing, by the way, something people do for TikTok or whatever? To actually make a run at the side panel of a bus stop?

M: I think everything is a thing now.

H: The first treatment of it is very dark. We've just had the tenth anniversary of the 2011 riots and it made me think of that.

M: In *To the Old World*, the second video, the feel has changed a lot. It has become much more about transcendent moments. He's basically trying to smash his way through to the other side. He's trying to port it himself, trying to port from one place to the other.

H: At the centre of a lot of what you do are experiences of ecstasy that come out of a very mundane reality. It's what makes your presentation of club culture so moving. People got to know you through *Fiorucci Made Me Hardcore* and that was all about transcendence. That video had a powerful sense of why people live for Saturday night, why people live for the club, why after you've been doing whatever dull thing you've had to do all week, going out and getting off your head on a dance floor is such a transcendent experience. In the new video, the guy runs at the bus stop. He comes out of our world and he falls into an abstract sparkle night space, where the sparkles are sort of fantasy stars but also what used to be called 'Islington diamonds', shards of smashed glass.

M: I think there are two things that attracted me to it. One is kind of autobiographical. I did something very similar when I was a youth. There was a period when I went through very nihilistic, drunken wrecked behaviour. It was really familiar to me and I'm

2. FIORUCCI
—
Elio Fiorucci (1935–2015) was an Italian fashion designer and founder of the eponymous Fiorucci empire. The label became synonymous with the best nightclubs worldwide, along with their associated excesses, and the title of Leckey's 1999 film *Fiorucci Made Me Hardcore* was taken from a piece of graffiti seen in a photograph of Studio 54 from the late 1970s.

3. MARK FISHER
—
British writer and cultural theorist who died in 2017, best known for the blog *k-punk*. Still readable at k-punk.org or in print anthologies. Fisher's insights on culture, politics and the intersection of the two remain more relevant to today than most things written yesterday.

always looking for these surrogate moments that I can occupy and put myself into. Any video I make, in some sense, becomes about a frustration with images, really, about their influence, how enthralled I am by them, the spell that they bind me with. I can't say I don't like it, because obviously I do, but there's a conflict in me about that and about its effect on me. I think it's interesting, what you say about the riots, and this idea of from the mundane to the ecstatic, because it's also a moment of violence. And I think, besides that, there's a kind of idea that any representation of violence is violent in itself. That's what I was circling around. He's directly running at the bus stop. And I'm indirectly trying to talk about other things or let the image carry other ideas about violence, about class, about a kind of male nihilism or kind of self-annihilation.

H: In the *Twilight Sparkle* version, the darker one, a scary voice intones part of a Ted Hughes poem called 'Wodwo': *But what shall I be called am I the first / have I an owner what shape am I what / shape am I* … The speaker in that poem is the green man, the wild man of the woods, and he's just coming to some kind of self-consciousness. And you link it to that 'male nihilism', the pointless destructiveness of the bus stop video.

M: 'Wodwo' I went to because I was looking for something, I was delving into a kind of British folklore and I came across that. I didn't know it before.

H: Does that link to your horror interests? There's a real resurgence of interest in the UK in what is now called folk horror. People are writing about it as a genre, a kind of cultural production — of films and books mainly, but also music, that mines a kind of atavistic sense of place, sometimes linking it to a feeling of being haunted by a lost past. Mark Fisher wrote a lot about this. Is he someone you're interested in?

M: Yeah. I used to read his blog, *k-punk*. I didn't know it was him for a long time. I actually met him and didn't know he was *k-punk*. Really I came to Mark posthumously. I came to him very late, but I've read all his books. And yeah, they're very important to me, especially his book *The Weird and the Eerie*.

H: That's been a useful book for me as well. And it gives a particular context to those lines of Ted Hughes. It brings out their mystical darkness. Do you read a lot of poetry?

M: Again, gleaning. I've just done a radio show where I played a clip of Kevin Killian. Do you know Kevin Killian?

H: I haven't read him.

M: Dodie Bellamy? Anne Carson?

H: Sure.

M: The gallery I'm with, Cabinet — Martin McGowan, who runs it, began as a poet. He is continually introducing me to poetry. He'll send me paragraphs that he knows will have some effect on me. So that's really useful. Pierre Guyotat was the last one he was trying to get me into.

H: You did a sort of lecture performance called *The Long Tail* that took as its starting point Chris Anderson's book of the same name. Anderson describes how the internet has made it possible to sell low volumes of lots of niche products, like for example literary books or art movies. But you link that to all sorts of things: to the history of media, to the first TV broadcasts and to the ideas of the British cyberneticist Gregory Bateson. How did you come across all that?

M: How did I come across... See, the thing with *The Long Tail*, a lot of these things, is I get completely absorbed with them, and once I've processed them, it's kind of gone.

H: You must have had to read Bateson's *Steps to an Ecology of Mind* to make that work.

M: More gleaning! I made *The Long Tail* in 2009. It was the moment of the emergence of the smartphone and I felt very disorientated by it, by the magic of it and how responsive it was to my desires. It seemed that it was generating a kind of feedback loop that we're familiar with now, this algorithmic desire, all our desires being instantly met. So I wanted to understand where the long tail had come from.

H: The piece gets kind of mystical. It's not just about you being able to access hard-to-find media. You talk about the long tail as a place where you live, where you exist, and then it begins to bleed into this idea that the long tail is offering you things, just everything you could imagine, that there's something symbiotic about the relationship, something a little scary. There was a sense that there are risks, that you can get to a point where that servicing of your desires begins to be weird.

M: The first thing I was looking at was the Chris Anderson book. And he introduced me to the culture around *Wired* magazine. To Kevin Kelly. And then Stewart Brand and the *Whole Earth Catalog*s. And then that led me to Bateson. I looked at Norbert Wiener and all that, but Bateson was completely fascinating. Tragic too in the sense that those ideas were never realised. So, yeah, I was just trying to

4. WHOLE EARTH CATALOG
—
A countercultural magazine from California, the *Whole Earth Catalog* by Stewart Brand was an exhaustive compendium of useful 'tools' for living ranging from carpentry utensils to early synthesisers. Steve Jobs later described it as 'Google in paperback form, thirty-five years before Google came along.'

Top: *O' Magic Power of Bleakness*, Tate Britain, London, 2020. Bottom: *UniAddDumThs*, Kunsthalle Basel, Switzerland, 2015

Both: *Containers and Their Drivers*, MOMA PS1, New York, 2016, photographs by Pablo Enriquez.
Find details of Leckey's current and future exhibitions at cabinet.uk.com.

understand. I'd never do it again, I kind of hated it after I did it in a way, because it's like... It's just Wikipedia.

H: But I watched it the other night and I think it stands up really well. You get the sense of one person putting all these different things together, but you've also got the theatrical aspect. You're a showman, putting on a performance, drawing on the chalkboard like a professor.

M: No, I guess it's the information. I don't hate it, but it's the... I don't know. It seemed quite new at the time. I'm still totally fascinated by the long tail. I think it remains true in a lot of ways. The art world at the moment is very 'long tail'. It's all about concentrated power in the head, aggregated power below. So I think the long tail is a useful way of understanding the world. In the nineties I was involved in a space on Clink Street in London called Backspace—

H: I used to go down to Backspace.

M: Backspace was fantastic. Do you remember James, the guy who ran it?

H: Yes. I knew James quite well, and there was the Ninja Tune guys in the building and I did stuff with them. There was an amazing energy around Backspace.

M: Definitely. There was another group, were they called Tomato?

H: They were designers.

M: I used to do coding. I used to do HTML. I did American Express's website, me and one other guy in like '96.

H: God. We were clearly in the same room a lot around that time, because I was down at Backspace all the time because I was working at *Wired* magazine and the office was just off Tooley Street, it was a short walk away.

M: Yeah. I mean I was basically bumming off James, that's why I was there. It wasn't very glamorous. It felt like — well, how I imagine the art labs in the sixties. That countercultural energy. And I still think those things have potential. Though I think it's hard now to look back at the narrative of countercultural liberation as anything but a kind of neoliberal emergence. I mean, look what happened. I was making a website for Amex.

H: There were people in the scene who were really trying to not get co-opted. All the net.art people I used to know back then who were determined to stay outside the mainstream. That whole scene had a very strong DIY ethic. It had the best part of the rave culture, which

5. TOMATO
—
A design collective of sorts, Tomato started life in 1991 as an undefined collection of creative individuals and has gone onto produce work for Nike, Coca-Cola and the European Commission. Founding members include Karl Hyde and Rick Smith, who are better known as electronic musicians Underworld.

Previous Page: All Images: courtesy the artist and Cabinet, London

was: we're going to clear a space, we're going to make it our space, and we're going to make the tools and the social relations that we want within this space and see if we can grow it to a point where it scales up. And of course what we all discovered is that at a certain point, the cool gets kind of skimmed off and sold to Microsoft or whoever, and the people who are really committed to the social experiment stay in the margins. There are a lot of people who did amazing work who I think don't recognise anything of what they did in the new culture of NFTs or whatever tech art, art on the internet, means now.

M: Like Jodi. Jodi.org. I was very into them. I thought they were amazing.

H: I liked them too. All those *Doom* levels they made that were just abstract spaces. I remember running through white noise, static basically, with my rail gun, thinking, 'This is amazing, they've hacked this very violent first-person shooter game and made something psychedelic out of it.'

M: I was trying to think of more books to recommend to you. Do you know this book *Darryl*, by Jackie Ess, have you heard about this?

H: No, I haven't heard of it.

M: Seems interesting. [It's about an Oregon man exploring the cuckolding lifestyle.] I would have more to recommend to you but all I'm reading right now are these weird Substacks about the deep forest and the GAFA stack and all this stuff.

H: What is the GAFA stack?

M: The GAFA stack is a great phrase. I use 'the GAFA stack' too much now. It's Google, Apple, Facebook, Amazon. And basically the argument is that you can't be countercultural if you're on any of these platforms.

H: Your output is owned by them?

M: There's this idea of going into the deep forest, which is basically going into the dark web and creating these decentralised places. It's basically all supported by fans, a shared culture.

H: So, whose Substack is talking about that stuff?

M: I don't know. I just come across these weird ones. I go down the tree and either I save them or I don't. I was reading this one and it's about this thing I'm really into at the moment — I can't find any of this now, but I can send you the link — and she's using Auto-Tune to talk about TikTok and how it's so beautiful and how we all live in TikTok. But there's something about it that just, it just feels very…

6. SUBSTACKS
—
Substack is an online platform designed to monetise newsletter subscriptions. Subscribers can search for their favourite, pay a monthly fee, and receive in-depth explorations on a specified theme direct to their inbox. Top of Substack's featured list at the time of writing: 'The Sword and the Sandwich', a newsletter by Talia Bracha which "juxtaposes in-depth essays on white nationalism and extremism with weekly features on notable sandwiches".

it's heartbreaking, what she's saying, I can't quite fathom it. But I'm kind of obsessed with it at the moment. I get most of my information from Twitter now, to be honest.

H: Same. I use it to keep up with all sorts of weird subcultural conversations. I like listening to people talking to each other who have professional expertise in something that I don't know about. Because even if I don't fully understand, I can listen to the *way* they talk to each other. I get a lot out of that. Maybe knitting Twitter is having an argument about knitting. I can get a lot out of eavesdropping on these little worlds that I wouldn't be part of otherwise.

M: That sounds like what I should do, because I follow a lot of very depressed people. But yeah, I think I said this to you the other day, this is a transformative shift in cultural thought. And basically I go onto Twitter to educate myself in it, because my peers don't know it.

H: I agree. If I didn't go and root around in the weird bits of the internet, I wouldn't understand how things are changing.

M: I do feel I sometimes curse this trajectory that we've been talking about, this kind of countercultural interest from the age of thirteen or fourteen. It now has me somewhat trapped, do you know what I mean? I want the pipe and slippers, I want to go into the garden. I don't want to be doing this any more.

H: You don't want to be watching random TikToks.

M: No.

H: I feel like I've done a lot of manic gathering, and maybe it's coming to a point when what I should do is sift the stuff I already have, and not worry too much about gathering even more new stuff. I mean, re-reading, rather than reading, just trying to understand all the inputs I've already had. Maybe that's an honourable project for a gentleman of a certain age.

M: Yeah. I think it is, isn't it. I have to look away. I have to find some way of looking away.

HARI KUNZRU is the author of six novels, including *White Tears* and *Red Pill*. He is a regular contributor to *Harper's* and *The New York Review of Books* and is the host of the podcast *Into the Zone*. Since he spoke to Mark Leckey, he's found a copy of Leckey's ten-inch record *Exorcism of the Bridge @ Eastham Rake* and is trying to work out if it contains hidden messages when played backwards.

Supernatural Bookshelf

Leckey's reading recommendations have a seven-to-four ratio of otherworldly to actually quite worldly.

COME CLOSER (2003)
Sara Gran

An eerie, tightly wound and succinct novella outlining architect Amanda's disintegration, tiptoeing the fine line between out-and-out horror and unsettling supernaturalism. Is she possessed by the demonic, or suffering a mental breakdown? 'Hypnotic,' says Bret Easton Ellis.

GOOD NEIGHBOURS (2021)
Sarah Langan

Set in Long Island, *Good Neighbours* is an utterly chilling dissection of sleepy suburban lifestyles; Langan is a three-time Bram Stoker Award winner and this, her newest novel, maintains her reputation as a master of the form. Interesting trivia in horror pedigree terms is that Langan's husband, J.T. Petty, wrote the *Outlast* video game series

ALL THINGS CEASE TO APPEAR (2016)
Elizabeth Brundage

A tale of two families, one old farmhouse and several untimely endings in Upstate New York. The book spawned Netflix's 2021 film *Things Heard & Seen*, starring Amanda Seyfried and James Norton.

THE LAST HOUSE ON NEEDLESS STREET (2021)
Catriona Ward

A darkly gothic novel centred around a dilapidated residence on the edge of a forest. Children disappear and are searched for. Much of the book is narrated by a religious cat named Olivia.

SISTERS (2020)
Daisy Johnson

The second novel by the youngest Booker Prize nominee in history (Johnson was just twenty-seven when her debut, *Everything Under*, was shortlisted in 2018) follows two siblings, July and September, through their adolescence in the isolated North York Moors. What happens tests sorority to deeply unsettling limits.

THE ANIMALS IN THAT COUNTRY (2020)
Laura Jean McKay

Given that McKay's novel concerns itself with the fallout from a global pandemic, the mere timing of its publication seemed virtually paranormal. That said, this pandemic seems less destructive than the IRL one, on surface level at least: one of its symptoms is the ability to understand animals, who prove to be complex, almost metaphysical linguists.

THE LAMPLIGHTERS (2021)
Emma Stonex

Inspired by the real-world disappearance of three Hebridean lighthouse keepers in the early twentieth century, Stonex's debut is equal parts murder mystery, ghost story and psychological horror.

THE HOURS HAVE LOST THEIR CLOCK (2021)
Grafton Tanner

On the power of nostalgia. How when a citizenry is forced to look headfirst into a bleak future, political leaders have capitalised on the resulting ache for the past, with often terrifying consequences.

THE MELANCHOLIA OF CLASS (2021)
Cynthia Cruz

With reference to cultural icons such as Amy Winehouse and Ian Curtis, Cruz examines the choice faced by all members of the working class who wish to break into the middle-class world that controls the culture industry: assimilate or be annihilated?

YOU'RE HISTORY (2021)
Lesley Chow

Subtitled *The Twelve Strangest Women in Music*, a riotous deep-dive into the psyches and sensibilities of a dozen female recording artists — from Rihanna to Kate Bush and from Shakespears Sister to Azealia Banks — in the pursuit of pure sonic pleasure.

HERMITS AND ANCHORITES IN ENGLAND, 1200–1550 (2019)
edited by E.A. Jones

Exhaustive account of the solitary and devoutly religious fellows once found throughout medieval England. Note the key difference in the lodging of an anchorite and his hermitic brethren: anchorites remain in one place (think anchor, like a ship) whereas a hermit is free to roam.

THE HAPPY
READER

A Study of Provincial Life

Winter 2021 — Issue nº 17 — Part Two

Welcome To Websville

Everyone is connected in *Middlemarch,* our Book of the Season for winter 2021/22, but often in ways they know nothing about.

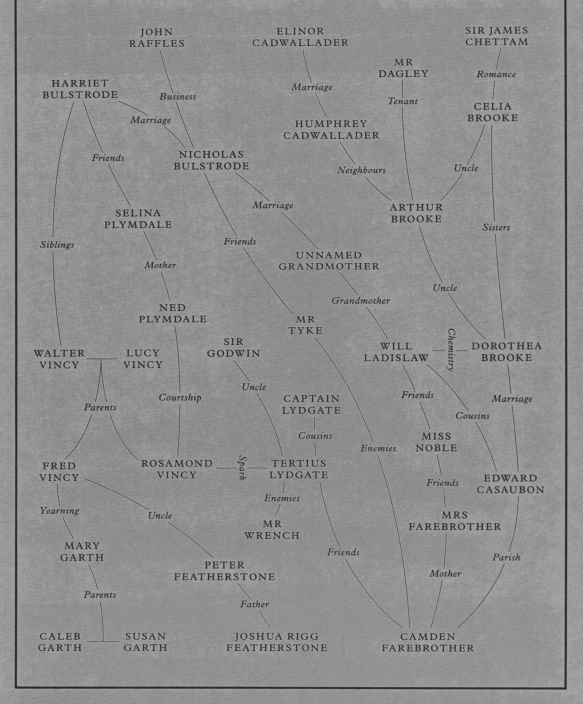

JOHN RAFFLES

ELINOR CADWALLADER

SIR JAMES CHETTAM

MR DAGLEY

HARRIET BULSTRODE

Business

Marriage

Romance

Marriage

Tenant

CELIA BROOKE

HUMPHREY CADWALLADER

NICHOLAS BULSTRODE

Friends

Neighbours

Uncle

SELINA PLYMDALE

Marriage

ARTHUR BROOKE

Friends

Sisters

Mother

UNNAMED GRANDMOTHER

Siblings

Grandmother

Uncle

NED PLYMDALE

MR TYKE

WILL LADISLAW

Chemistry

DOROTHEA BROOKE

SIR GODWIN

WALTER VINCY

LUCY VINCY

Uncle

Friends

Marriage

Courtship

CAPTAIN LYDGATE

Cousins

Parents

Cousins

MISS NOBLE

Enemies

FRED VINCY

ROSAMOND VINCY

Spark

TERTIUS LYDGATE

EDWARD CASAUBON

Enemies

Friends

Yearning

Uncle

MR WRENCH

MRS FAREBROTHER

MARY GARTH

Friends

Parish

PETER FEATHERSTONE

Friends

Mother

Father

CALEB GARTH

SUSAN GARTH

JOSHUA RIGG FEATHERSTONE

CAMDEN FAREBROTHER

If anyone has tried to exhaust *Middlemarch* it is RE-BECCA MEAD, who has written countless essays, given a TED talk, and published a bestselling memoir about her lifelong obsession with the novel. But now, in a world of upended social norms, Mead finds it has yet more to offer — as any true classic must.

George Eliot Reads The News

When London, where I live, first went into lockdown on account of the coronavirus pandemic in March 2020, and the stay-at-home order permitted just one period of outdoor exercise per day, I sometimes went to a hillside park in the neighbourhood of Highgate, in north London. There, I could look down across landscaped lawns upon the city, suddenly silenced but for the wail of ambulance sirens, and traverse paths marked with signs warning me and other visitors to maintain two metres' distance from each other. On these outings I often saw an elderly man who took a walking stick with him on his own perambulations, fiercely brandishing it out to his side with a rigid arm to mark the limits of his personal airspace whenever anyone else passed by.

It was a terrible, fearful time — a beautiful, death-haunted spring. I could also see, though I could not enter, Highgate Cemetery, which lies adjacent to the park, separated by iron railings. The cemetery, which opened in 1839 when Highgate still had the character of a village some distance from central London, is one of London's best-known and most beautiful burial places, now thickly wooded with trees and populated with mossy gravestones, though once its high prospect was open. Its most celebrated deceased occupant is Karl Marx, whose tomb is marked by a massive bronze bust, bearded and craggy, beneath which the words 'Workers of All Lands Unite' are engraved and picked out in gold upon a marble pedestal. At the onset of the pandemic the cemetery had been obliged to lock its gates. But it was easy to see Marx's tomb from the perimeter of the park, his enormous head glowering through the branches.

My eye, though, always wandered to another, less prominent monument a few hundred paces away: an obelisk among the tree trunks and gravestones. This is the tomb of George Eliot, who was laid to rest in Highgate Cemetery on a bleak, rainy day at the end of December 1880, at the age of sixty-one, dying after taking ill at a concert a few days earlier. It was this tomb that had been the reason for my first visit to Highgate Cemetery a few years ago, when I was researching a memoir, *My Life in Middlemarch*, about my decades-long love of and engagement with George Eliot's greatest novel. My introduction to *Middlemarch* was at the age of seventeen, and I returned to it every five years or so thereafter, my understanding and appreciation of it growing and changing with every revisiting. What I could not have anticipated was the way in which, in those early months of 2020, an entirely new dimension of the novel came into focus: the looming spectre of the cholera epidemic, which struck England in 1832.

Middlemarch is set at precisely this moment: in Book Six of the novel, the narrator remarks that in and around the town, 'railways were as exciting a topic as the Reform Bill or the imminent horrors of Cholera'. The Reform Bill of 1832, in which the franchise was extended, 'rotten boroughs' were dissolved, and the privilege of the landed gentry in England was extended at least partially to accommodate the interests of a rising middle class, is an important theme in the novel, even if it is one that a contemporary reader unversed in

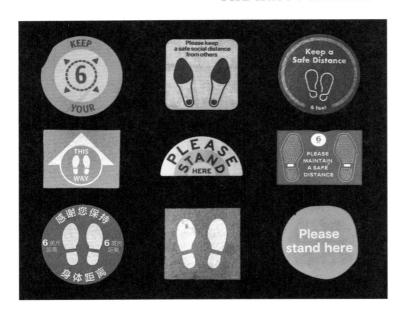

Assorted social distancing iconography from 2020.

Image: Savannah Walker, *Six Feet Apart Please*, 2021

nineteenth-century history is perhaps likely to skim. Meanwhile, the novel's treatment of the advent of the railway line cutting through the hitherto sleepy meadows around the town of Middlemarch signals Eliot's interest in transformational technology and its effects upon the established rural order.

Railways and politics: these are aspects of life in the Victorian era in England which, in the first decades of the twenty-first century, still seem proximate. But the threat of cholera — a pandemic disease which spread for the first time from Asia to the rest of the world in the 1820s — seemed until recently to be entirely redolent of a bygone era, though Eliot had witnessed four epidemics by the time she published *Middlemarch* in 1871. Despite a reader being told that cholera is the third principal topic of chatter in the taverns and the meeting rooms of Middlemarch, it's a dimension of the novel that is only lightly touched upon. Cholera is explicitly mentioned fewer than ten times in the entire book. Existing as a threat but not as a condition, it is easily overlooked — at least until one finds oneself in the midst of a pandemic, with new rules to observe, and new terrors to be haunted by, and new losses to assimilate.

But cholera does make its mark on the narrative of *Middlemarch*, and George Eliot's notebook for the novel, in which she recorded factual ballast for her invention, is filled with transcriptions from medical journals and other sources about the disease and its mitigation. Sanitary provisions are being made to protect Middlemarch, while a ward of the hospital has been prepared in readiness for those stricken by the disease, which was characterised by a rapid onset of diarrhoea and vomiting and could kill within hours. One character in particular is especially associated in Eliot's narrative with cholera: Nicholas Bulstrode, the wealthy, pious banker whose fortune has been built on an ill-gotten inheritance.

Bulstrode's exposure as a hypocrite and a thief — and, ultimately, as partly responsible for another individual's death — swells in significance as Eliot's novel progresses towards its conclusion. Bulstrode, who is about sixty, and whose physical appearance is repeatedly described as sickly, is one character in the novel who admits to a sense of vulnerability: 'I presume that a constitution in the susceptible state in which mine at present is, would be especially liable to fall a victim to cholera, if it visited our district,' he says to Lydgate, the ambitious doctor, a new arrival in town, who has, against his better judgement, found himself socially and professionally aligned with the unpopular Bulstrode. A meeting is called at the town hall to discuss the creation of a dedicated burial ground to accommodate the epidemic's anticipated fatalities; but before the meeting gets under way, however, the other board members call upon Bulstrode either to refute the rumours of his transgressions or to step aside. Bulstrode rises from the table and staggers, only to be assisted by Lydgate, who sits alongside him and who, as a human and as a doctor, feels compelled to offer his support, though doing so confirms the false suspicion that he is a willing enabler of Bulstrode's corruption. ('What could he do? He could not see a man sink close to him for want of help,' Eliot writes.) In the discussion about a burial ground, Bulstrode's own reputation is buried, while Lydgate becomes the unfortunate victim of Bulstrode's moral contagion.

One of the terrible consequences of our own pandemic has been the reframing of human proximity as a threat. If the elderly man brandishing his stick as he walks in the park next to Highgate Cemetery were to stumble, would my grasping of his arm be understood by him — and even by others — as a dangerous incursion, rather than a gesture of care? We have learned to regard our neighbours as potential vectors of disease, rather than as bestowers of support. As I walk around the park — and even, these days, go into the cemetery, which is once again accepting visitors — I find myself giving others a wider berth than once I would have done, making a perverse gesture of solidarity through increased distance.

In considering how we will come through this reshaping of our social encounters, and what symptoms of our sickly relations with each other may linger, it is worth remembering what George Eliot wrote of Bulstrode, whom she consistently refrains from judging: 'He was simply a man whose desires had been stronger than his theoretic beliefs, and who had gradually explained the gratification of his desires into satisfactory agreement with those beliefs.' As always in *Middlemarch*, Eliot goes on to urge her readers towards sympathy with others. 'There is no general doctrine which is not capable of eating out our morality if unchecked by the deep-seated habit of direct fellow-feeling with individual fellow-men,' she observes. These words are even more necessary now, when the conditions of our fellowship have been so challenged, and we all walk within sight of the graveyard, warding off the fear of death.

REBECCA MEAD is the author of *My Life in Middlemarch*, a New York Times bestseller, and the brand new memoir *Home/Land*. She has been a staff writer at the *New Yorker* since 1997, and a resident of London since 2018.

MEMOIR

Read it, wait for a while, then read it again. Keep doing this. Forever. No novel has more lifetime acolytes than *Middlemarch*. Here's how ROB PALK describes his initiation into the club.

My Twenties, My Thirties, My Forties…

I am in my twenties and my life is about to change. I am about to finish *Middlemarch* for the first time. I am about to walk out on a six-year cohabitation because someone keeps bringing me cake. I'm not saying there's an absolute relation between these life-altering events, but they seemed closely linked at the time. I knew what success looked like, in my twenties. It was the noughties and success looked like warehouses in east London full of thin women in large belts. This wasn't the life I led. I lived in south London with a nice schoolteacher and worked a

1. MEN
—

One summer's day at the start of this decade, a group of men walked up to a statue of George Eliot in Nuneaton and stood there in a way that said, 'we are on guard'. The impetus was a desire to protect the monument from the wave of statue removals then allegedly on the rise. Except Eliot, a vocal opponent of slavery and antisemitism, was an unlikely target, and it was just another baffling episode from the rising culture wars.

boring job. Only someone at this job kept bringing me cake.

The cake-bringer worked in the same large charity office as me, in the room next door to mine. Three or four times a day she brought me offerings: cups of tea, wedges of lemon drizzle, occasionally books. When she brought the tea, she stood above me and we talked. Silence rippled out along the workspace. People pretended, not very skilfully, to be occupied. The cake-bringer's skin turned a pinker colour. The cake-bringer wore a heavy perfume and, when I drank from the cup she had brought me, her scent lingered in my hands. She was friends with people in bands. She had 'done' some modelling! She often went to Berlin. She was the success world made flesh. I wanted this. She was reading *Middlemarch* and so I read it too.

I know: I should have read it before. I thought of it as the sort of book my sister liked: fat, with a black spine, all big houses and governesses and crinoline and squabbles over inheritances. Books I liked were thin, with blue-green spines, and featured chain-smoking men having melancholy affairs in hotel rooms with drunk women called Yvonne. I also knew that *Middlemarch* was supposed, in a vague way, to make you a Better Person, like vitamins or yoga or going to Bali. I didn't want to be a better person and maybe this put me off.

The first thing the book brought: a deep immersion, the sort you normally lose in adult life. I was *there* in Tipton Grange, I could smell the stables and the dust on the jewellery boxes, hear the papery swish of dresses in motion. The next step was feeling, as we didn't say in the noughties, *seen*. More than any other author, George Eliot seemed able to lift the lids of our heads and take a look around. This had a quelling effect. Somehow this author knew everything. No vanity escaped her. She knew what it was to be young and ardent and have no outlet. She knew what it was to let your better urges get hobbled by weakness. She knew what it was to be a sceptical but conscientious vicar or a guilty Methodist banker, a husband who marries an idea. She would pop up every few pages or so and tell us what to think, and somehow this wasn't annoying but the best part of the book. She knew about men. Boy, did she know about men. She knew about failure. There were so many ways to fail. You could come a cropper in middle age for the crimes committed in youth. You could be reckless or unwise in love. You could fail to speak out on minor injustices, fail to challenge prejudices or challenge the wrong ones. You could let 'spots of commonness' override your better plans. You could drift from arty dabbling to worthwhile cause and back again, never finding your path. You could be Casaubon. This was the scariest fate, a character seemingly made up of homilies and old parchment until, in one of the great record scratches in literature, Eliot stops the action and shows his soul, shows us someone we could be, if we buried ourselves in futile projects, if we let our fear of failure confirm us in our failing.

The book cast the whole world of success into doubt. Perhaps this was how it made you better. I loved it but I didn't feel any improvement. If anything, I thought, if messing up is so inevitable, so ingrained, then what's the point of fighting it? I stopped feeling guilty about the cake-bringer. One day I left my home and partner and ran to the cake-bringer's side. I was experiencing Frenzy and this was important. I would move to east London, be a Creative Young Person with

Enticing Victorian
cake styles.

her, I would drink in draughty bars furnished with old sofas, I would pass fashion shoots on the way to work, the success world would be mine. She dumped me after a week. This was an experience too.

I am in my thirties and it is time to read *Middlemarch* again. Many things have gone wrong, not all of them my fault. Some of them are my body's fault. A few years earlier, I had an enormous stroke. Some veins in the back of my brain were tangled and exploded. You feel a bit more vulnerable, after that. You lack elan. My marriage has just ended. I had married someone in the success world, someone glamorous, a friend of artists and film-makers. I felt on the way to arriving. Only it turned out she didn't care for any of that. There was a gulf between what she symbolised and who she was, and somehow I'd failed to spot this. I was still in the same job but about to be made redundant: I would probably have to leave London. The success world had escaped me; it had seen me coming and fled. I was seeing a refugee from another scuppered relationship. Her ex had been a struggling artist or had at least mastered acting like one. The experience had given her a righteous fury against male entitlement. I was thrilled by her denunciations of my sex, while hoping I was partly excused from them.

'My God, it's him,' she said. 'It's my ex.' She was reading *Middlemarch* and had got to Casaubon, his pedantry, his nervous vanity, his hopeless labours. I hoped I was more like Will Ladislaw, an amiable, faintly bohemian dabbler. She told me I should read the book again. I obeyed. I was doing a lot of obeying. I had got a lot of life wrong and taking instruction from her seemed a useful way out of this. Although maybe asking for instructions was a further imposition, I wasn't sure. Either way, I found my old copy.

This time round, I felt the anger. I noticed Dorothea, born with too much energy for her age, energy which she throws into being Casaubon's wife, the amanuensis for a bookish husk, into minor schemes for social improvement and eventually a happier marriage. None of these activities felt quite enough for her. I noticed the chorus of small-town

2. DOROTHEA
—
Because the eighth track on Taylor Swift's *evermore* album is called 'Dorothea' there has been speculation as to whether it's about the heroine of *Middlemarch*. Except Swift's Dorothea is 'a queen selling dreams' in the form of 'make up and magazines' which doesn't sound like Eliot's Dorothea at all.

decision-makers who surround her, trying their best to regulate her into being just like them. Despite her temporary wealth and opportunities, Dorothea's seemed like the real tragedy of the book. It was the tragedy of not having enough to do, of having limitless energies and nowhere to put them. I wondered how a book so completely successful could contain such an understanding of failure. Dorothea struck me as key to that. She was an Eliot who hadn't elbowed her way to London, an Eliot who hadn't been advantageously unattractive to dreadful men, an Eliot without an outlet. The age she lived in, which on my first read had seemed a pleasant enough place, now seemed an enormous conspiracy to prevent Dorothea from flourishing. Even Will Ladislaw, the man she loves, seems only to be the best of a bad bunch. How can this picturesque dilettante, with his fondness for singing and his half hearted commitment to radicalism, measure up to Dorothea's high seriousness? How could anyone? It's a struggle to think of who could make a suitable love interest for our heroine — John Stuart Mill? Oliver Cromwell? — but much as we root for Ladislaw, it's hard to shake the suspicion he doesn't quite make the grade. Dorothea is simply too big for all that surrounds her.

I was chastened. I wanted to go round apologising but I wasn't sure who to. I tried the woman I was seeing. She said it was fine, she had a weakness for 'thwarted men'. 'The whole thing wants burning down though,' she said. 'Just burn down all of it.' I agreed, hoping this didn't mean she would dump me. Soon afterwards I lost the job and left London and got ready to live on a different scale.

I have just turned forty and finished another read. Turning forty is odd. I keep expecting a crisis that hasn't arrived yet. Maybe midlife crises kick in later these days, now that we're living longer. What happens instead is I wake up early and think *You're forty* and a strange jolt goes through me. *I am an adult*, I say to myself, but don't believe it. I live in the Midlands now, not far from where Eliot began, and I write and don't have much cash. My girlfriend used to be part of the world I wanted to join, back in my twenties: she acted, rehoused the homeless, opened squats and was briefly a master chocolatier. The crash came in 2008 and the world got meaner and smaller. There was a collapse in expectations. She found a job in a library, which now fulfils most of the roles abandoned by the welfare state. She guides people through their forms, she reads to children. For both of us, the success world seems very far away. The world has got tougher and attempts to make it less so seem, for the moment, to have failed. Getting up in the morning seems like an achievement enough. Unexpectedly, we are happy. The other day the children who use the library drew pictures of their inspirations and one of them chose her. 'The growing good of the world,' said Eliot, 'is partly dependent on unhistoric acts.'

On this read, I notice the happiness. It's a clear-sighted happiness (Eliot never lets us forget that one of the most likeable characters, Mr Brooke, is also a terrible landlord) but, for all that the book is a great fume against the forces that throttle promise, it's also more than that. Virginia Woolf said that Jane Austen wrote 'without hate, without bitterness, without fear, without protest, without preaching'. Leave aside the preaching and the same can be said of Eliot. This doesn't make a

3. FORTY
—
Turning forty this year: film star Dan Stevens aka *The Happy Reader*'s cover star for its first issue back in 2014.

Image: Alamy

MIDDLEMARCH FROM THE AIR
The town of Middlemarch is a fictional version of Coventry, a city in the English Midlands around thirty miles southeast of Birmingham. In the spring of 2020 the European Union's Copernicus Sentinel satellite passed over Coventry, taking this photograph as it went.

comfortable fit with our times, when books are expected to come heavy with protestation. Equanimity looks too close to conciliation. But reading *Middlemarch* again, it feels like a miracle. Eliot was able, not just to live on her own terms in a world that was hardly friendly to abnormally clever, God-doubting, wedlock-flouting women from the provinces, but to paint a picture of this world that makes life seem entirely worth living.

This time what stays with me isn't just Dorothea's frustrations, the townsfolk's instinctive resistance to change or even to individuality, or the chaos the principal players make of their marriages, but the atmosphere of the billiards room in the inn, Dorothea's sister's pride in her baby, the unexamined decency of their neighbours, the way Will always lies on the rug when visiting houses, Dorothea's earnestness in conversation, and the way the book depicts transcendent eruptions of love and lust. Somehow Eliot writes about a tragic society, a society weighted against people like herself, and manages to write with love. Life is unbearably sad, unbearably unjust, and still absolutely worth the cost. To think this and to encapsulate it in a text seems a moral as much as an artistic accomplishment. Or perhaps this is just how it feels to me, turning forty. For me the book's most affecting scene is when Mrs Bulstrode looks at her husband after he admits his wrongdoing to her. Mr Bulstrode is the book's version of a villain out of Dickens, a respectable puritan sinner, a hypocrite and thief. And, in a moment Dickens couldn't have written, his wife looks at him with full understanding, and forgives and loves him all the same. You can do the same for life, I think. You can look at the muddle and mess of it, the folly and frustration, and do so with forgiveness and love. You don't even have to be a genius, as Eliot was. Maybe this is what they mean, when they say *Middlemarch* improves you: not your deeds, which are as silly as ever, but the way in which you live with them.

ROB PALK is the author of *Animal Lovers*. He hopes to work on his second novel for a lifetime, growing more and more paranoid about its worth, eventually dying with it unfinished. He has read *Middlemarch* far too many times.

In honour of virtuous Dorothea Brooke, JEAN HANNAH EDELSTEIN recalls her own past as a good person that others would do well to imitate.

Some Times I Set A Good Example

I was born to set a good example. Or so I have been told. Before a group of freshly post-partum women in a hospital maternity ward, I was taken from my mother's arms by a nurse to be used as the model for a demonstration of baby bathing. My mother insisted that my great beauty was the reason I was selected to set an early good example, but photographs (while faded) reveal that when I set my first example, I was just another baby: squashy and red-faced.

I set a good example as a small child, when we were in a public place. 'We're in a public place!' my mother would say, at any hint of behaviour that was not a good example, and, conscious of the need to set a good example, I would cease. I set a good example in public places and I didn't even believe in God, and believed only a little bit in Santa Claus, instead fearing the retributions of the public, their judgement, which I imagined to be acute. I set a good example for the public, as if the public cared.

I set a good example on the German class field trip, to Amish Country, in central Pennsylvania. We visited a mocked-up Amish farm, and we toured a pretzel factory. I set a good example in an Amish-themed restaurant where I ate fried chicken with good manners, with a knife and fork, and all the other children pointed at me with fingers greasy from eating with their hands. I set a good example with my cutlery handling, and the other children laughed. Later, when our chaperones had settled us in our motel rooms, they placed strips of masking tape on our doors to prevent us from sneaking out to kiss the boys from German class. I set a good example, and my masking tape remained intact.

I set a good example as a teenage anti-drug role model. The other teenage anti-drug role models and I were taken to visit a classroom full of younger students, answering questions as a panel. 'Have you ever used drugs or alcohol?' one of the younger students asked, and one by one the other anti-drug role models replied, 'Yes. Yes. Yes.' 'No,' I said. I set a good example, and I could hear one of the younger students whispering to the student next to them, 'That one is a nerd.'

I set a good example when the fire alarm went off, in student halls. The fire alarm went off because someone burned some toast (we were not allowed to have toasters: burning toast did not set a good example). As the alarm pealed, I knocked on doors to tell my hall mates that we had to leave; they looked at me with bleary eyes from problem sets or marijuana, disinclined to follow my example. I set a good example when it came to fire safety, but on the day when the firefighters were actually called (a candle set some curtains alight) I was taking an exam. 'Oh,' said my friends, as they stood outside, watching the building that we lived in smoulder, 'if only Jean was here to see it. She set such a good example.'

I set a good example at the party. Which party? All the parties, when I was young, and there were always parties. I set a good example because I did not take drugs (because I was

too afraid of drugs) and I went home when I got tired, before dawn. 'I'm going home,' I'd say, and I'd set a good example of departure, of good sense and sleep hygiene, and then everyone at the parties went on having fun without me and the good example that I'd set.

I set a good example at the office. 'Who is not washing up their coffee cups in the office?' I asked the other people in the office, and the other people demurred. As a good example, I stood in the kitchen and scrubbed the cups and loaded them into a dishwasher with a flourish. When no one paid attention to my splashing, I made a sign about the coffee cups: *These coffee cups do not wash themselves*, the sign said. I had it laminated. I set a good example at the office, and the CEO emailed my boss and said he found the sign passive-aggressive and wanted it taken down.

I set a good example on a plane. It was a 6am flight, and I got there early, but the window seat was taken by a woman who was the last person on the plane. As the plane took off she shifted in her seat, uncomfortable. 'I need to go to the bathroom,' she said, with an air of desperation. I pointed at the seatbelt sign, which was turned on. 'The seatbelt sign is on,' I said, 'it is not allowed.' And I thought, *Perhaps you should have gotten to the airport earlier, and restricted liquid intake*. I set a good example with my adherence to the rule of the seatbelt sign and mild dehydration, and at last the woman did a muffled scream and climbed over me while the plane accelerated upwards. I set a good example and nearly made a woman wet herself.

I set a good example to my son. 'I am going to eat these beets because they are on my plate,' I said, 'they are so delicious! We are so lucky to have beets!' I set a good example, and I ate the beets with gusto, and my son laughed at me and threw his portion to the dog. I set a good example, and my son was two years old. I set a good example, and the dog also didn't care for beets.

JEAN HANNAH EDELSTEIN is a writer who studies life in provincial New Jersey.

Middlemarch, 2022

The characters of *Middlemarch* are rendered with such empathy that we can look into a modern crowd and say to ourselves: there's a Dorothea, there's a Caleb, there's a Will. That's partly because George Eliot describes the characters down to their very eye colour, but also because, over the course of 838 pages, we come to understand those characters more fully than many of our actual family and friends. *The Happy Reader* proposes the assemblage for an imagined TV remake or film adaptation, nine contemporary faces with the energy of the world's favourite fictional Midlanders.

Photography by
MARTON PERLAKI

Casting by
BEN GRIMES
TIAGO MARTINS

Styling by
FLORENCE ARNOLD

WILL, on page 35
Artist with a mysterious past. 'I have a hyperbolical tongue: it catches fire as it goes.'

ROSAMOND
Her excellent education creates new ways to be dissatisfied. 'I would rather not have anything left to me if I must earn it by enduring much of my uncle's cough and his ugly relations.'

CASAUBON
The more he works on his book, the less finished it becomes. 'My mind is something like the ghost of an ancient, wandering about the world and trying mentally to construct it as it used to be.'

DOROTHEA
Wishes the world would simply let her improve it. 'People are almost always better than their neigh-bours think they are.'

MRS BULSTRODE
Always dropping by for a chat. 'I never saw the town I should like to live at better, and especially our end.'

CALEB
Very reliable. 'There's no sort of work that could ever be done well, if you minded what fools say.
You must have it inside you that your plan is right, and that plan you must follow.'

MARY
Sharp wit and a beautiful heart. 'I will never engage myself to one who has no manly independence, and who goes on loitering away his time.'

FRED
Job seeker. 'I don't make myself disagreeable; it is you who find me so. Disagreeable is a word that describes your feelings and not my actions.'

LYDGATE
Doctor and gossip magnet. 'I have made up my mind to take Middlemarch as it comes, and shall be much obliged if the town will take me in the same way.'

Two friends reread *Middlemarch* across the space of several months. One is the literary critic DEBORAH FRIEDELL; she swaps notes with famous actress JORDANA BREWSTER, known for her role as Mia Toretto in the *Fast & Furious* franchise, among other movies. Former room-mates from college days, they're excited for an excuse to read Eliot again.

Book Club With Old Friend Who Happens To Be A Film Star

Since graduating university, Jordana and I had often talked about having a book club together. A few times we got as far as settling on a novel — *Effi Briest*, *Magic Mountain* — but never made it to the first chat. Work intervened, or families. We needed someone else to impose a deadline. Enter *The Happy Reader*. Jordana had last read *Middlemarch* as a student. And although I had prided myself on rereading *Middlemarch* every few years, I realised that, actually, it had been at least a decade since my last attempt — I couldn't quite remember what Bulstrode had done to disgrace himself, or how Casaubon was related to Ladislaw. And I wondered how I'd experience the story differently now that I was closer to Casaubon's age than to Dorothea's.

(ONE) I Zoomed with Jordana from her study in Los Angeles. My trip to visit her had been cancelled by the pandemic, but I've seen pictures in *Architectural Digest*. It's huge and gorgeous, with bookshelves out of the library sequence in Disney's *Beauty and the Beast*. She was with her fiancé, Mason Morfit, and I could hear her two small sons in the background. I was in my north London flat, at my kitchen table slash desk slash everything else.

DEBORAH: I'm so sorry that the *Fast & Furious* London premiere was cancelled! I was looking forward to stealing all the mini toiletries from your hotel suite again. I just used up the last soap from the time you stayed at Claridge's.
  JORDANA: I think I'll still be coming in January though. Can you hold out until then? Let me know if I need to mail you some shampoo.

D: And we can do a George Eliot tour? Her house in St John's Wood is no more, but we can still walk by her mansion on the Chelsea embankment. Michael Bloomberg owns it now.
  J: I'm sure he's read all of her novels.

D: Do you remember how you felt about *Middlemarch* the first time you read it?
  J: I read it more in earnest. I wasn't so jaded. It was before my first marriage. I'm not sure that I even realised that Dorothea is headed

4. A KEY TO ALL
MYTHOLOGIES
—

In an interview with
Vulture, Franzen describes
the trilogy's title as being
linked to (1) an in-joke
with his partner; (2) the
inescapable nature of
religion; and (3) 'the
fact that Casaubon dies
in *Middlemarch* before
he finishes his project.
And undertaking writing
three books in my 60s,
I thought, "Well, that's
a funny little joke."'

towards disaster. Here's the quote I highlighted: 'Dorothea's faith
supplied all that Mr Casaubon's words seemed to leave unsaid: what
believer sees a disturbing omission or infelicity? The text, whether of
prophet or of poet, expands for whatever we can put into it, and even
his bad grammar is sublime.' That's what gets us into so much trouble:
she'll just fill in with her own imagination. She doesn't even wonder if
he's good enough for her; she just worries that she's not good enough
for him. So many hints on rereading that I didn't pick up on the first
time around. And then I went and made the same mistake that she did.

D: Susan Sontag said she sobbed when she read *Middlemarch* — she
realised that the professor she'd married at seventeen was a Casaubon.

J: 'The mistakes that we male and female mortals make when we
have our own way might fairly raise some wonder that we are so fond of
it' — I love that. What's interesting is that Dorothea really is more at
fault than Casaubon: he didn't pretend to be something he wasn't, but
she envisions a partner who isn't there. Would Dorothea make a much
better match if she didn't choose for herself?

D: If someone like Mrs Cadwallader was put in charge?

J: What if the reader chose for her — how good a job would we do?

D: Henry James can't have been the only reader annoyed that Dorothea
didn't end up with Lydgate. He couldn't stand Ladislaw. What am I
saying? The truth is that I always want them to end up together too —
of course Dorothea would have supported his fever research.

J: I wonder if Eliot is deliberately trying to get us to play matchmak-
er. Also, Dorothea totally leads Sir James on — I don't believe that she
doesn't know what she's doing.

D: Have you read Jonathan Franzen?

J: Only *The Corrections*.

D: I'm supposed to be reviewing his new novel. The whole reason I
agreed to write about it is that I thought there'd be some *Middlemarch*
connection, because it's part of a trilogy called *A Key to all Mythologies*.
The only thing I can think of — I worry this is too much of a stretch
— is that *Middlemarch* was almost a historical novel for George Eliot —
not like Mary Renault, not about ancient Greece, but she was looking
back about forty years. And the Franzen novel is set in the 1970s, so
it's as though he's looking back almost the same amount of time.

J: Maybe there isn't a connection. He's pretty self-aware. Do you
think it's probably just a joke at his own expense?

D: Probably. When someone asked George Eliot about the real life
model for Casaubon, she pointed at herself. The way he spends years
organising all his papers into pigeonholes, and wondering if it's to any
purpose... I see what you mean. That's probably how all writers feel.

J: Listen to this: 'Don't you think men overrate the necessity for hu-
mouring everybody's nonsense, till they get despised by the very fools
they humour?... The shortest way is to make your value felt, so that
people must put up with you whether you flatter them or not.'

D: My younger self underlined that too! But how exactly — particularly if you're a woman — without being a grande dame?

J: It's very Hollywood. I've seen this with X — don't use her actual name when you write this up. She always acted as if she was the most deserving of all the perks, and she absolutely manifested it into reality. But I always felt underserving and would beg my lawyer just to settle for the first offer. Don't forget to let me know if there's ever a novel you think I should option. I just keep thinking about Gillian Anderson at the Emmys — I want a career like hers, that kind of trajectory, resurrection. I need to take more control.

(TWO) We arranged to talk again in a week, after we had both made it to Book 5. But Jordana had to travel across the country for a funeral, and then for work, and after a few weeks we still hadn't been able to schedule another Zoom. But I wasn't too worried. And I loved waking up to the text messages she often sent me about what she was reading.

J: I LOVE this passage: 'This is a very bare and therefore a very incomplete way of putting the case. The human soul moves in many channels, and Mr Casaubon, we know, had a sense of rectitude and an honourable pride in satisfying the requirements of honour, which compelled him to find other reasons for his conduct than those of jealousy and vindictiveness.'

J: It raises the question: do we delude ourselves non-stop to satisfy our ego? Is there any way to escape this delusion? For example, in MY MIND, I know why I got divorced. To a spectator (or anyone who reads comments on the *Daily Mail*), I'm a jezebel who jumped from one man to another.

J: Coincidentally, I was in Maine attending my aunt's memorial service while I was reading about Featherstone's funeral. The contrast was remarkable. Whereas F had a bunch of hangers-on attending, hoping to get something, the tent at my aunt's memorial was filled to the brim with actual mourners — ranging from her children to the man who coached her now thirty-year-old son's soccer team when he was in middle school.

D: I thought your tribute to her on Instagram was beautiful — actually sort of *Middlemarch*-ish: even though she wasn't famous, she made so many lives better, like Dorothea's unhistoric acts.

J: I loooooved ladislaw's letter to casaubon

J: Telling him to fuck off

J: Just a small thing, but she's so good on how certain memories get affixed to places and imprinted in our memory.

J: 'Will not a tiny speck very close to our vision blot out the glory of the world, and leave only a margin by which we see the blot?' Again! How beautifully does George Eliot express how self-centred and bothersome

---

5. GILLIAN ANDERSON AT THE EMMYS

When Anderson won Best Supporting Actress last year for her portrayal of Margaret Thatcher in *The Crown*, she accepted the award in a silk two-piece dress adorned with tiny metal penises.

6. DAILY MAIL

Brewster is a mainstay of the *Daily Mail*'s celebrity coverage, attracting a story roughly every two weeks on subjects such as the fact that she's on the beach, or her latest purchase of a cup of coffee.

we are to ourselves? I know there is a better way to put that... Perhaps some comparison to Covid and how that would 'fix' our perspective and make us appreciate all that we have but as soon as life returns to normal, BOOM! We are back to being our petty selves.

J: 'Was it her fault that she had believed in him — had believed in his worthiness? — And what, exactly, was he? — She was able enough to estimate him — she who waited on his glances with trembling, and shut her best soul in prison, paying it only hidden visits, that she might be petty enough to please him. In such a crisis as this, some women begin to hate.'

J: AGAIN, the power of self-delusion! Shutting her truth in 'her best soul in prison'... pretending to be something less strong, less wonderful than what she actually was... of course she would 'begin to hate'.

J: But the interesting question is: is it all Casaubon's fault? Didn't Dorothea delude him into thinking she was a fawning fan?

D: I keep thinking about Lydgate's 'vocation' scene — when he falls in love with anatomy. Would we feel differently about Casaubon if we had a similar moment for him, in flashback? He must have had a moment when he fell in love with scholarship, or was it always about ego? So much of his coldness to Dorothea is bound up in his feelings about his work — he thinks she's judging him as the world judges him (and as he judges himself).

J: Let's chat tomorrow. It's much, much more difficult to read when I'm at home. The kids demand a lot. Headed to the Dominican Republic, so I should have more time to read. Also shooting a film in NYC in November.

(THREE) After a few weeks, we still hadn't arranged a last call, and I was beginning to worry. When we finally connected, I was desperate to ask her about wedding planning, but time was limited, and we made an effort to stay on track.

D: Hello! Do you want to switch to Zoom?
J: I just got on the plane to Santa Barbara.

D: Why Santa Barbara?
J: To meet with the wedding planner!

D: Oh wow. We need to talk about that, but *Middlemarch* first. How do you feel about Lydgate and Rosamond?
J: Don't you think Eliot glossed over their courtship — particularly compared to how she describes Dorothea's?

D: I love how in Victorian novels — but also in *Sex and the City* — the more space is given over to wedding preparations, the more you know the marriage is likely to be doomed.
J: Will try not to take that personally.

7. SANTA BARBARA
—
The best bookstore in the sunny sleepy Californian city is almost definitely Chaucer's Books at 3321 State Street.

D: I'm struck by how sympathetic I am to Rosamond this time around
— I don't like it! I know that when I read the novel twenty years ago,
I wanted to strangle that swan neck. And now — well, am I project-
ing my twenty-first-century feminist self onto the text, or is George
Eliot with me? — I can see that Rosamond's 'quiet elusive obstinacy' is
pretty much the only card she has. Lydgate has a life outside the house,
but she doesn't. He tells her nothing about their finances, and then it's
suddenly: *we're in debt and you have to leave the house*. But the house is
all she has. Of course she doesn't want to leave it.

J: Lydgate sets her up. She went to charm school, but he expects
her to know enough about medicine to admire his genius, or just to
take him at his own self-assessment. I think it makes sense that you're
softening towards her — we're getting older. You saw things as more
black and white then. A girl who just went past me must think we're
gossiping about real people.

D: What do you make of Ladislaw?

J: I highlighted the bit about his 'magic touch' — how a man's
passion for one woman differs from another; morning light versus
Chinese lanterns. It's beautiful. But my favourite couple in the book
are definitely Fred and Mary: they're the most honest. They accept
each other's flaws.

D: Is Ladislaw realistic? For extra credit I looked at Rebecca Mead's
memoir-ish book about *Middlemarch* — she has a whole section on
how dismissive the early critics were about Ladislaw. They called him
'a schoolgirl's dream', and argued that George Eliot had fallen in love
with him herself but that she didn't quite make him credible. Do they
have a point?

J: What? No! Why?

D: I mean, he reminds me of someone I know! A failed PhD student
who went to work for the Bernie Sanders campaign. Was he too modern
for the early critics?

J: So what if Ladislaw was her own fantasy? Good for her!

D: Would you want to be in a movie version of *Middlemarch*?

Speed Read

The eight original instalments of *Middlemarch*, roughly summarised with mild spoilers

Book 1
MISS BROOKE

An enigmatic yet compelling conversation about jewellery. Dorothea Brooke refuses to marry James and, against advice, accepts a proposal from Casaubon instead. Old Featherstone hears Fred is being vocally presumptuous about inheriting all his money. Fred, meanwhile, procrastinates about gambling debts and yearns after Mary.

Book 2
OLD AND YOUNG

Lydgate make a compromise involving local philanthropist Mr Bulstrode so as to be put in charge of the new fever hospital. In Italy with Casaubon, Dorothea realises their life together is less fulfilling than she'd hoped. But when she crosses paths with Will, there is a palpable chemistry.

Book 3
WAITING FOR DEATH

Fred tries to solve his debt issue by making a deal involving a horse. It's a disaster. The whole thing falls back on the Garth family. Casaubon collapses. Lydgate and Rosamond get engaged. Featherstone dies after asking the only person nearby, namely Mary, to help burn one of the two wills he wrote. She refuses, as it wouldn't be proper.

Book 4
THREE LOVE PROBLEMS

Will is staying with Mr Brooke. Casaubon is suspicious that he just wants to be close to Dorothea. Featherstone's money, which would have gone to Fred if Mary had burned the will, instead goes to an illegitimate son named Rigg. Brooke buys a newspaper. Mary's father Caleb gets a new job.

Book 5
THE DEAD HAND

Rosamond is pregnant. Lydgate's way of doing medicine attracts suspicion. Casaubon dies, leaving a clause in his will forbidding Dorothea to marry Will. Brooke is heckled during an election speech. Raffles, an old business associate of Bulstrode, shows up, hinting at dark secrets from the past.

Book 6
THE WIDOW AND THE WIFE

Dorothea hires Caleb to manage the estate and he has a stand-off with villagers unhappy about a rail-line. Fred discovers that Mr Farebrother, who he'd asked to speak with Mary on his behalf, is himself in love with her. Rosamond miscarries. Will learns important truths about his own history.

Book 7
TWO TEMPTATIONS

Rosamond looks for a solution to their financial woes and it backfires. Raffles is back, spreading rumours but also very ill. Bulstrode calls for Lydgate to act as doctor, also agreeing to lend him a large sum of money. In the morning, Raffles is dead. Ruinous gossip spreads across town.

Book 8
SUNSET AND SUNRISE

Rosamond's dinner invites are declined. Dorothea tries to help but walks in on Rosamond and Will in a compromising position. Mrs Bulstrode sticks by her husband. Dorothea comforts Rosamond, who absolves Will, who goes to see Dorothea. Mary says yes to Fred. Final sentence about unhistoric acts and the growing good of the world.

J: Not a movie — too many storylines — but a miniseries or TV show. And update it, so that it's not a period piece. I'd take the cast from *Mean Girls*: Rachel McAdams as Dorothea and Amanda Seyfried as Rosamond.

D: In a small university town, with Casaubon as a professor. Bulstrode is the university's major donor. Caleb Garth is in charge of the grounds. But does the story work in an age when women can get jobs? Wouldn't Dorothea want a career of her own — be a professor rather than just marry one?

J: You always wanted to marry your professors! Fred could lose money on cryptocurrency rather than a horse. Rosamond stays the same: she thinks she's marrying a rich doctor, not a researcher with lots of student loans. They're closing the doors now. I'm going to have to hang up in a second.

D: We need to talk about the ending. Is it quietly tragic, even if Eliot didn't intend it to be? We don't see scenes of Dorothea and Ladislaw married — but hear of her nearly dying?

J: I'll text you!

DEBORAH FRIEDELL is a contributing editor of the *London Review of Books*. She lives across the street from where George Orwell wrote *Keep the Aspidistra Flying*.

In honour of stubborn yet indecisive Mr Featherstone, YELENA MOSKOVICH devises a small fiction in two acts.

Two Wills, Burn One

I bequeath my worldly possessions as follows: my last painting and a half-used acrylic paint tube (Chiffon White). This is how I painted it. I got my wooden easel and my brushes and my big linen canvas and all my acrylic tubes (I find oils too *voilà*) and set up camp at the edge of what I'll humbly call my garden, then I set my house on fire. I waited as the flames grew and whiffed about the rooms and cracked through the glass of the bedroom window. I studied it with my most sensual focus, a round 12 brush between my teeth. I painted away. Slops of paint, smeared and smoothed with my whole heart. The paint rose into the brush hairs, crawled up the wooden base, seeped into my fingertips, through my palms, grasped my wrists and pulled me inside. The painting is called *Burning Home*. I give it to the one who burns to come home.

I bequeath my otherworldly possessions as follows: Couch potatoes. Cancelled plans. The wood lily I would have liked to find in the impromptu forest eight minutes from the train station. My short end of the stick. The ghost my cat kept chasing in her midnight furies. The heat from the hot hot shower when I took hot hot showers to humidify the accumulated interpersonal despair. Also, if I'm emptying my pockets, unwarranted hope. Feral tenderness. The secrets I kept, despite the fact that I found them petty. That awkward squawk from the slow pigeon I ran over accidentally with the heavy city bike. It was missing a leg. Now it's missing its whole body. The roll of good luck and the roll of bad luck and the dice in the mirror. The chain of curses at the terrible rain. It was terrible. Closeness. Wetness. Shivers. Shudders. Sneezes. Regrettable grins. Candid farts. Ears that finally pop. And that warm – hot – burning – feeling between solace and woe. I give it to the one who can never come home.

Choose one of these wills and burn the other. You can't have both. You rarely can.

YELENA MOSKOVICH is the author of three
novels (and two wills), who also draws and paints
vulgar and sentimental things.

SELF-CARE

An ode to following one's erotic urges honestly; or how Casaubon, the driest of scholars, the pompous failure of a husband, struck TARA ISABELLA BURTON (and many like her) as nothing less than the ideal man.

Education Sex

Back in July 2020, when the pandemic was bringing new levels of derangement to inboxes and Twitter feeds across the country, the *Slate* advice column 'Dear Prudence' (aka Danny Lavery) published a very particular sex-help question. The letter writer had been reading *Middlemarch* with her boyfriend, she said, and the two of them shared a fascination with one of the novel's least erotically obvious characters: the pompous, elderly professor, Edward Casaubon, Dorothea's ill-matched and ill-fated first husband. The letter writer's boyfriend, in search of a new kink to spice up their sex life, proposed something he called 'solemn play' — in other words, 'pretending to be like Casaubon toward Dorothea, refusing sex and making her instead do long, pointless tasks for him... rife with erotic sublimation'.

Whether or not this letter was a hoax — 'Dear Prudence' attracted many — it does get at something real about Casaubon's appeal, as baffling to many readers as to Dorothea's shocked and worried contemporaries. Casaubon may be 'no better than a mummy' and 'a great bladder for dried peas to rattle in' (to quote Dorothea's horrified friends and family); but he's also — at least to Dorothea, and to those readers, like myself, who identify with her on this point — deeply sexy. For, although Dorothea protests that her primary interest in Casaubon is to 'help' him in his 'life's labour', her desire for him is, though not explicitly sexual, nevertheless an erotic one. It is a hunger for a certain kind of transformation. It is the culmination of all of Dorothea's many earlier renunciations in the novel: she relishes, for example, giving up her late mother's jewellery, and her pleasure in horseback riding. She decides to marry him not just despite but because of her friends' and family's horror of her decision. She decides to marry him, in part, to blow up her life, to enter an intimate world whose standards are so unlike the ones she is flaunting by entering it.

'Her whole soul was possessed by the fact that a fuller life was opening before her,' George Eliot writes, describing Dorothea receiving Casaubon's proposal, 'she was a neophyte about to enter on a higher grade of initiation ... allowed to live continually in the light of a mind that she could reverence.'

It is precisely this fantasy of transformation that made me identify so intensely with Dorothea, and, in particular, the rebellion in her decision to marry a man everyone else in her circle did not just despise but disdain. Reading *Middlemarch* for the first time in my early twenties, I too — despite myself — developed a crush on Casaubon, as well as on his real-life analogues. (I often fantasised about writing *Dorothea seeking her Casaubon* on my dating-app profiles, although I never quite got up the nerve.)

It wasn't simply the hot-teacher fantasy, nor was it solemn play as kink. Rather, it was the fantasy of renunciation as a kind of total surrender: a surrender that, though erotic in nature, would encompass the totality of my life, both inside and outside the bedroom. It was the fantasy of finding a partner who would shape me, and in whom and through whom in turn I could become someone blessedly unlike myself.

Although I never quite married a desiccated professor many years my senior, I continually sought out in my personal life people I thought of as moral superiors. They were the people who, I believed — by virtue of being older, or more religiously observant, or more rigid about rules — would tell me how to live, who would give meaning and shape to my existence. I, like Dorothea, fetishised renunciation, ached for the sacrifice of certain kinds of pleasure, took delight in my own abasement as the baby, the student, as one who needs to learn how to be a person.

For me, the pragmatic element of this — the desire to learn how to be somebody else — and the sexy element of it — the desire for surrender as an erotic phenomenon — converged. Both, ultimately, derived from my hunger for intensity, for a life purer and richer and better and more saturated with significance than the ordinary life I lived outside this erotic spell. Both promised entrance into an enchanted world, equal parts boudoir and cloister.

It is that hunger that lies at the heart of both Dorothea's spiritual quest and her romantic one. Dorothea's story is erotic not in the prosaic sense of wanting to have sex with Casaubon, but in the sense that she learns to understand, and discern, her own desires. Her inchoate longing for something more, something outside herself, something transformative and world-shattering and self-shattering, sheds light on the nature of desire itself, and the way desire for another, in the sexual sense, and for transformation, in the spiritual sense, are often indistinguishable from one another. What Dorothea wants, in the end, is to be overcome. Maybe, Eliot suggests, that's what we all want too.

Maybe what we all want is to be destroyed and remade, in the image of something better. What could be sexier than that?

TARA ISABELLA BURTON is the author of *Social Creature: A Novel* (2018); *Strange Rites: New Religions for a Godless World*, and the forthcoming novel *The World Cannot Give* (2022). She is working on a history of self-creation, to be published in 2023.

PROFILE

Mary Ann Evans, better known as George Eliot, was born in the Midlands in 1819. She published eight novels plus countless essays, poems and translations, including one of Spinoza's famous philosophical treatise, *Ethics*. Her love life made the romances of *Middlemarch* look simple: as Lena Dunham once put it, 'George Eliot's Wikipedia page is the soapiest most scandalous thing you'll read this month.'

Letters

To polish off a book from either end

Hi there Happy Reader,

Tim Blanks writes that he begins reading every novel with the last sentence ('On the Last Sentence', *THR16*). The problem with this method is that endings tend to be the worst part of any book — the action has faded, the sentiment rises, the family finally sits around the table for a Norman Rockwell-style Thanksgiving, happily ever after, the end. What makes a good ending anyways? Novels are complicated little-big things and the last sentence is the worst to write, the final chapter the most tedious. I often don't read the last pages at all but rather loosely scan, flipping through, anxious to put the book back on the shelf and grab a new one. It may not be for the lazy, as Tim Blanks describes himself, or for those with horrible time-management skills, but the best way to know if a story is worth your time is to start from the beginning.

With love,
Nathaniel Feldmann
Amsterdam

Dear The Happy Reader,

I was interested to learn of Walt Whitman's death mask being held at Princeton ('Snippets', *THR16*), and it has compelled me to bring a rather less terrifying aspect of Whitman to the attention of Happy Readers. During the pandemic I realised reading Whitman was the perfect antidote to isolation anxiety. His self-appointed role as the poet of everyday people stands in contrast to the way life's ever-accumulating decisions cause us to become ever more solipsistic. During lockdown, as we shared our newly humdrum lives and confronted the new intangible ways of doing things (customers and salespeople talking through plastic screens; colleagues talking through phone and laptop screens), Whitman's joyous calls to carpenters, boatmen, mothers, wood-cutters, shoemakers et al felt like a celebration of all the quotidian and banal work I was doing, as each of us were. Should you be struggling with refinding your pace (and place) within society at large, I recommend a Whitman poem or two (preferably read aloud, if you can bear to do so). It always sorts me right out.

Yours sincerely,
Bella Gladman
London

Dear Seb,

Reading about the words different languages use to identify bibliophiles ('Snippets', *THR16*) opened a long-overlooked door in my memory. I'm standing in a room deep within the library at the University of Sydney with the rest of my English class and our bespectacled lecturer, looking at: incunabula, gently laid out, creamy-faced and seeming to sigh slightly when the librarian turns a page. Her gloved fingertip pointing out a tiny, delicate constellation of holes left by the passage of an actual medieval bookworm. And I've never seen sign of one since: do bookworms still exist? Perhaps they don't have an appetite for modern books?

Yours faithfully,
Rosie Findlay
London

Letters for the summer issue must be received no later than 1 March 2022 and sent to the following email address: letters@thehappyreader.com.

The next Book of the Season, which readers are encouraged to finish before July, is Nella Larsen's iconic Harlem Renaissance novel *Passing*.

Summer Book Reveal

In the 1920s and 1930s, the Harlem neighbourhood of New York City became a centre for Black creativity. Billie Holiday, Aaron Douglas, Duke Ellington and many others rose to prominence within the movement known as the Harlem Renaissance — as did the author Nella Larsen, whose landmark novel *Passing* is our Book of the Season for summer 2022. Published in 1929, it tells the story of a pair of mixed-race friends, Clare Kendry and Irene Redfield, who live on either side of the 'colour line': the legal and social wall separating white and Black people during segregation. Clare has built a life as a white woman, even while America's so-called 'one-drop rule' meant anyone with even a single African ancestor was considered Black in the eyes of the law. Her act of 'racial passing', unknown to her deeply racist husband, leads to tragic consequences.

Larsen drew on her own mixed-race heritage to write *Passing*. Its delicate exploration of racial ambiguity remains relevant today, and the book has duly acquired the status of a classic. Last year *Passing* was adapted into an acclaimed film by Rebecca Hall.

SUBSCRIBE

Each issue of *The Happy Reader* combines an expansive conversation about reading with an attempt to magazinify a single classic book. Subscribe and never miss an issue by visiting boutiquemags.com.

To receive the monthly newsletter from editor-in-chief Seb Emina please visit thehappyreader.com/newsletter.

Jacket for *Passing*, originally published in 1929.